The
Magic Coin

by Ruth Chew

illustrated by the author

SCHOLASTIC INC.
New York Toronto London Auckland Sydney

ISBN 0-590-40779-1

12 11 10 9 8 7 6 5 4 3   0 1 2/9

To my nephew

Jean-François Foucar Chew

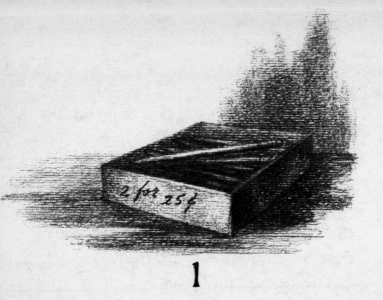

1

"Sorry, young lady, this isn't any good." The man behind the counter handed back the coin Meredith had given him.

"The sign says pencils are two for a quarter," Meredith told him.

"But that isn't a quarter." The store man turned to help a lady who wanted to buy a box of envelopes.

Meredith put down the pencils she was holding.

"What's the matter, Meredith?" Christopher asked.

Meredith set her book bag on the floor of the store. She showed her brother the coin. "I thought it was a quarter."

Christopher took a good look. "It's the same size as a quarter. But everything else about it is different."

The store man leaned over the counter. "If you aren't going to buy anything, kids, why don't you go outside?"

Meredith picked up her book bag. The two children went out of the store onto Church Avenue.

"Where'd you get that coin?" Christopher asked.

"They didn't have the paper at the corner candy store this morning," Meredith said. "Daddy sent me to the newsstand on McDonald Avenue to get one."

"That's more than four blocks from

our house," Christopher said. "Weren't you late for school?"

"I ran all the way," Meredith told him. "Daddy gave me a half-dollar and said I could keep the change. I'd better go back and tell the man at the newsstand he made a mistake."

"Let me see it again." Christopher reached for the coin.

Meredith handed it to him and started walking down the busy Brooklyn street.

Christopher looked first at one side of the coin and then at the other. He turned it on edge. "I can't see any copper in it. Maybe it's all silver."

"Then it's worth more than a quarter." Meredith started to walk faster. "I've got to give it back." She looked around. "Hurry up, Chris."

"Instead of an eagle," Christopher said, "there's a shield on the back. And the face on the front isn't at all like the man on the quarter."

"George Washington is on the quarter," Meredith reminded him. She waited for her brother to catch up with her. "Let me see what you're talking about."

Christopher gave her the coin.

Meredith looked hard at the shield. "That's a coat of arms. It's what knights had."

She turned over the coin.

A man's face was on the other side. He had a trim little beard and wore a suit with a collar and a bow tie. Meredith remembered that on the quarter George Washington was wearing only a hair ribbon. You could see just one side of his face. This man was looking straight at Meredith and frowning.

"He doesn't look much like a knight in armor," Christopher said.

Meredith started walking faster.

At McDonald Avenue Meredith and Christopher crossed the street and went over to the newsstand.

Meredith showed the silver coin to the man there. "You gave it to me by mistake this morning," she said. "My change should have been a quarter."

"I don't know what you're talking about," the man said. "You didn't get that from me. Run along and don't bother me."

Meredith put the coin back into her pocket and walked away from the newsstand. "I wish that man hadn't been so nasty," she told Christopher, "but I'm glad I didn't have to give him the coin."

"So am I," Christopher said. "It's a nice thing to keep."

Meredith took out the coin again. Christopher grabbed his sister's arm. "Look!" he whispered.

Meredith stared.

The little bearded face on the coin was smiling!

2

Meredith was so surprised that she nearly dropped the coin. She couldn't take her eyes off the face of the little man.

The more she looked, the more it seemed as if the coin could never have been any other way than it was now. Both children kept looking at it. The face on the coin didn't move even a little bit.

Finally Christopher said, "It's funny. I thought he had an angry sort of face."

Meredith nodded. "To me he seemed worried. Now he looks happy." She thought for a minute. "Chris, we're being silly. It's the light that makes the coin look different."

It was still light out, but the sky was becoming cloudy.

"It's getting late. Mother must be wondering where we are. We'd better go home." Meredith started walking toward the corner of the street.

They turned onto Albemarle Road. It was a quiet street with big old houses on each side. Meredith and Christopher could go much faster here than on Church Avenue where there were crowds of people.

Pale green blossoms misted the branches of the maple trees. And little green buds peppered the hedges in the front yards. Meredith stopped to look at a yellow crocus.

"I thought we were in a hurry," Christopher said. "Mom's probably mad already."

Meredith felt a drop of rain on her cheek. Another one splashed on her nose. She was wearing her new spring coat. "I wish we had an umbrella."

Meredith remembered that she was still holding the silver coin. She tried to put it into her pocket, but it wouldn't fit. "Chris!"

Christopher turned around. "What's the matter?"

Meredith held up the coin.

It was as big as a saucer. And it was getting bigger!

At the same time the coin was getting
thinner. In a few seconds it was so thin
that the children could almost see
through it. The shield on the back
showed through and got mixed up with
the face on the front of the coin.

Next the edges curved down to make a big upside-down bowl.

The coin wasn't any heavier than before, but it was so big now that Meredith had to balance it over her head with one hand. She had her book bag in the other.

Meredith felt a bump on the underside of the coin. It sprouted down like a silver stem. She found herself holding onto it as if it were a handle.

Her brother stood next to her. The rain was pouring all around them, but they weren't getting wet.

Christopher and Meredith were standing under a big silver umbrella.

3

"You can't tell me it's only the light," Christopher said.

For a minute Meredith just looked up into the umbrella. "No, Chris. It isn't the light. It's magic."

"Magic or not, Mom's sure to have a fit if we're not home soon," Christopher told her.

Meredith started walking quickly along Albemarle Road. Christopher was shorter than she was. He had to run to keep up with her.

The rain was splashing all around

the umbrella, but even their feet stayed
dry. At East Fifth Street, Meredith and
Christopher turned the corner and hur-
ried to a house in the middle of the
block. They climbed the front stoop.

Christopher rang the doorbell.
"You'd better close the umbrella before
Mom sees it. She's going to ask us where
we got it. And she'll never believe what
we tell her."

"I don't know how to shut it," Meredith said. "It doesn't have any spokes, so how can it fold? I wish we had some way to hide it."

The umbrella seemed to shiver. The silver handle got shorter and shorter. In a second or two Meredith was once again balancing the big bowl on her hand. The bowl flattened into a plate, and the plate began to shrink.

Mrs. Dalby opened the door of the house. "You must be soaked." She looked at Meredith. "Why are you holding your hand like that?" She smiled. "Does it keep the rain off you?"

Meredith looked up. She was holding the silver coin over her head.

"Come in before you get any wetter." Mrs. Dalby pulled the children into the house. "Get out of your coat, Meredith. I'll hang it up for you."

Meredith put down her book bag and

unbuttoned her coat with one hand. She was holding the magic coin in the other.

Mrs. Dalby picked up the coat and went to hang it up. "It's not nearly as wet as I thought it would be," she said. "Bring your jacket here, Chris. And let's see your shoes."

"Do you think I should go in the kitchen and pour water over my shoes?" Christopher whispered to Meredith.

"Don't be silly, Chris!" Meredith said. But she too was wondering what she could tell her mother.

Mrs. Dalby hung up Christopher's jacket and looked hard at both his and Meredith's shoes. "The rain seemed to be coming down in buckets," she said. "How did you keep from getting wet?"

Meredith looked at the coin in her hand. The face on it was frowning at her. She took a deep breath. "We had a magic umbrella, Mother."

Mrs. Dalby laughed. "That explains everything," she said. "Come into the kitchen now and get your after-school snack before it's suppertime."

Meredith took another look at the coin.

The little bearded face was smiling again.

4

After supper Mr. and Mrs. Dalby settled themselves in the living room to watch television. Christopher sat on the floor next to his father's chair.

"Don't you have any homework, Chris?" his mother asked. "Meredith is up in her room doing hers now."

"Oh, I forgot." Christopher walked into the dining room to get his books off the buffet. Then he went upstairs.

Meredith's door was open. She was sitting at her desk working on her math. Christopher had never seen Meredith's pencil move so fast.

He tiptoed into the room and stood behind her. Meredith was doing a page of fractions. Christopher knew she hated them.

He watched Meredith copying numbers out of her math book. She leaned forward to look at something on her desk. A moment later she wrote some more numbers on her paper.

It seemed to Christopher as if some-

thing were giving Meredith the answers to her math problems. He craned his neck to see what it was. There was a pile of books on the desk. He couldn't make out what was on the other side.

"Meredith," Christopher said, "what's going on?"

Meredith turned around. "I'm beginning to understand fractions."

"What have you got on your desk that you keep looking at?" Christopher asked.

Meredith stood up. "Look."

Christopher leaned over the pile of books. He saw that Meredith had placed the magic coin right where the desk lamp would shine on it. The little bearded face looked up at Christopher.

"He seems to be asking what it is I want from him," Christopher said.

"That's just what I thought," Meredith told him. "And when I look at him for a little while, I understand what I have to do."

"How about lending me the coin?" Christopher asked. "You've been using it long enough."

"Come on, Chris, you know my homework's much harder than yours." Meredith picked up the coin. "You always want somebody to help you. I wish for once you could do your homework by yourself."

"Oh, all right." Christopher walked out of the room.

Meredith went on with her math. When she finished it she opened her social studies book. She used the coin for a bookmark.

The lesson was about Columbus and how he discovered an island and named it Little Spain. Meredith thought the magic coin trembled between the pages of the book.

It was an exciting story, but there were sad parts in it. When Meredith finished reading she felt as if she had been on the faraway island with the people who were greedy for gold and the other people who died working in the mines to get it for them.

Meredith took the silver coin out from between the pages and laid it on the desk top. Then she closed the book.

Christopher came back into the room. "Guess what," he said. "I did my spelling homework all by myself. And I'll bet I can spell every one of those words."

Meredith caught sight of the face on the coin. The little man was not exactly smiling now. He just looked very pleased with himself.

5

Next morning Meredith fell back to sleep after her mother called her. Mrs. Dalby was so busy trying to get Christopher up that it was breakfast time before she found Meredith was still in bed.

It was after eight o'clock. Meredith dived into her clothes and gobbled a bowlful of cornflakes. She grabbed her coat and book bag and rushed out of the door after Christopher.

They were two blocks from home when Meredith remembered that they'd left their lunch bags on the kitchen table. They ran back to get them.

"Hurry, children," Mrs. Dalby said.

"You'll be late for school." She went down the basement stairs with a load of laundry.

Christopher picked up his lunch. "What did you do with the magic coin?"

"I left it in my room." Meredith ran upstairs.

Christopher followed her. Meredith was in such a rush to grab the coin off her desk that she dropped it on the floor.

Christopher put his foot on the coin to stop it from rolling away.

Meredith bent down. She poked her fingers under Christopher's shoe to grab hold of the silver coin. "I thought taking it to school might help me with the math test," she said. "But it's only going to make us late. I wish there was some way we could get to school on time."

The room seemed to blur before the children's eyes. A minute later everything was clear again.

"Wow!" Christopher said. "Look at the coin!"

The silver coin was as wide as the kitchen table. Meredith looked across the room. Her bed was very far away. And it was the size of an apartment building.

The coin started to rise in the air. Christopher was standing on it. He sat down. Meredith climbed up beside him. She thought her weight would push the coin back onto the floor, but it just floated higher.

The silver coin sailed across Meredith's bedroom. Her window was open a crack at the top. The window was enormous now. And so was the crack. The coin slipped through into the open air outside.

Meredith put her book bag on her lap. Christopher tucked his books and his lunch between his knees. Both of them held tight to the sides of the flying coin.

Meredith looked over the edge at the streets and houses below. They seemed much bigger than they ought to be. "You know what I think?"

"What?" Christopher asked.

"Nothing really got bigger," Meredith told him. "We got smaller."

Christopher didn't have much time to think about this. "There's the school!" he yelled.

"Your class is already going in," Meredith said.

The silver coin flew down into the crowded schoolyard. It landed right beside Meredith's class.

The boys and girls looked like giants.

Meredith looked up at the biggest shoe she had ever seen.

Christopher grabbed his books and his lunch and jumped off the coin. At once he was as big as ever. He raced across the yard and followed his class into the school.

Meredith stood up. As soon as she stepped off the coin she was back to her right size. She bent down to pick up the little silver coin. Then she got on line.

Mrs. Fleming waved to her. "You're just in time, Meredith. I was afraid you were going to be late."

6

Meredith's class had to practice writing first thing in the morning. Then they took turns asking each other questions about yesterday's social studies homework.

At eleven o'clock Mrs. Fleming said, "It's time for our math test, boys and girls. Petra, I want you to give out the papers."

Meredith placed the silver coin face-up on her desk.

Petra walked up and down the aisles. She put a blank sheet of paper on each desk. When she came to Meredith's desk, Petra took a good look at the coin. "There's a picture of that man in one of my grandmother's books," she said.

"What's his name?" Meredith asked.

"I think it's Juan Pablo Something-or-other," Petra told her. "But I'm not sure."

Mrs. Fleming rapped on her desk with a yardstick. "Petra! Stop talking and finish your job."

"Yes, Mrs. Fleming." Petra gave Meredith a sheet of paper and went on to the next desk.

Meredith looked at the coin. The face on it was frowning again. Meredith remembered that Mrs. Fleming had a desk drawer full of things people had brought to class. There were a lot of baseball cards, several pea shooters and water guns, and at least one set of jacks in the drawer. Mrs. Fleming kept it locked. She was going to give the things back on the last day of school. That was almost three months away.

If Mrs. Fleming thought Meredith

was playing with the coin she might lock it up in her drawer. Meredith picked it up and put it back into her pocket.

"I'll just have to remember what I learned from Juan Pablo when I was doing my homework last night," she said to herself.

During the test she found that fractions were easy now that she understood them. The test was like a game. Meredith had fun with it. She was one of the first people to finish. Mrs. Fleming asked her to collect the papers when the test was over.

At twelve o'clock Meredith met Christopher in the big basement lunchroom of the school. They sat at one end of a long table.

The lunchroom was noisy. The voices of the boys and girls seemed to echo off the metal ceiling. Meredith almost had to shout to make herself heard.

"I found out his name," she said.

"Whose name?" Christopher asked.

Meredith pulled the coin out of her pocket and put it on the table. She placed one finger under the chin of the man with the beard. "His."

Christopher unwrapped a sandwich and bit into it. "Peanut butter."

"No," Meredith said, "Juan Pablo." She took a bite of her sandwich. "This stuff sticks to the roof of my mouth. I wish we had some milk to go with it."

Meredith felt something move under her finger. It was the coin. "Juan Pablo's getting bigger again."

Christopher stared at the coin. "We don't need an umbrella in here."

The coin spread out in all directions like an egg dropped into a frying pan. When it was a little bigger than two fried eggs, the edge of the coin turned up to make a rim, and the coin stopped growing.

"It's a silver tray," Meredith said.

"And look what's on it!" Christopher picked up a small container of milk and handed another to his sister.

Meredith pointed to the tray. "He even remembered the straws! Thank you, Juan Pablo."

7

The peanut butter sandwiches tasted good with the milk. Meredith and Christopher each had a yellow apple and two chocolate cookies packed in their lunch bags. The milk lasted just until they had finished eating everything.

They put the empty milk containers and the straws back on the little tray. A second later they were gone. The silver coin was once again lying on the table.

Meredith picked it up and put it into her pocket.

Today was Friday. The afternoon seemed to go on and on.

At last it was three o'clock. Meredith met Christopher at the gate of the schoolyard. They started to walk along Albemarle Road.

"I'm tired," Christopher said. "Why don't we fly home?"

Meredith took the coin out of her pocket. She placed it on the sidewalk. "We have to be standing on it."

Christopher looked at the man on the coin. "What did you say his name was?"

"Juan Pablo," Meredith told him.

"It seems pretty awful to step on his face now that we know who he is," Christopher said.

Meredith remembered what her mother said when she had to do something that would bother somebody. "I beg your pardon, Juan Pablo," she said and stepped on the coin. She could only get one foot on it, so she put the other foot on top.

She expected to shrink small enough

to sit on the coin, but nothing happened. "Please, Juan Pablo, fly us home the way you flew us to school."

Still the coin stayed just as it was on the sidewalk.

"Maybe something happened to the magic," Christopher said. "Or maybe he doesn't like being stepped on and has given up flying. See if he'll do something else."

Meredith hopped off the coin and stooped to pick it up. "Is there some other kind of magic you'd like to do, Juan Pablo?" she asked.

The coin just lay in her hand. The face on it looked straight at her, but there was nothing about it that was special. For a moment Meredith wondered if she'd dreamed all the magic.

"If we hadn't fooled around we'd be home by now." Meredith dropped the coin into her pocket. "Last one home is a rotten egg!" She started to run. Chris chased after her.

Meredith reached the house first. She went up the steps two at a time and rang the doorbell. Christopher came charging up the front stoop right behind her.

Mrs. Dalby opened the door. "I've never known you two to get home from school so fast. What is it, more magic?"

8

Meredith liked to do her homework on Friday. That way she didn't have to think about it for the rest of the weekend.

After supper she sat down at her desk. She took the silver coin out of her pocket and placed it where she could see the face on it. "Maybe you'll help me with my homework, Juan Pablo, even if you're tired of magic." Meredith opened her science book.

Christopher burst into her room. "How about lending me Juan Pablo? I decided to do my homework now."

"I wanted him to help me," Meredith said. "Why don't you wait till Sunday night to do yours, the way you usually do?"

"Please, Meredith," Christopher said.

Meredith looked hard at the face on the coin. "Oh, all right."

Her brother picked up the coin and went out of the room. Meredith closed the door and started to read her science book. She kept remembering the look on Juan Pablo's face. Somehow it made her think she ought to lend Christopher the coin.

She read a chapter on electricity and all the things it could do. It was quite a lot like magic, Meredith thought. When she closed the book she found that she remembered everything she'd read. She had to make up questions on what was in the chapter. Meredith told herself the answers as she wrote down each question.

Her math had never seemed so easy. The chapter in the social studies book came alive like a television program in her mind.

Meredith saved the homework she liked best for last. That was reading.

She finished her library book. Then she remembered that she had to do a book report on it. Meredith hated book reports. They almost ruined the fun of reading the books.

She took a fresh sheet of lined paper and started. "The main character is a girl who goes to live with her grandfather," she wrote. Meredith saw Juan Pablo's face in her mind. He was smiling. She smiled too and went on writing.

Her homework was finished before it was time for bed. Meredith put away her books and went to see if the magic coin was helping her brother.

Christopher's room was at the back of the house. Meredith went down the narrow hall. The door was open, so she walked in. Christopher was talking, but Meredith didn't see anybody with him.

"Why don't you just tell me the answers?" he said.

Now Meredith saw that Christopher was holding the coin in his hand and arguing with it.

"What's the matter, Chris? Didn't you get any help from Juan Pablo?" she asked.

Christopher looked up. "Oh, sure," he said, "I got all my work done. But this character makes me look in the book for what I have to know. I think he should just give it to me straight. It would save a lot of time."

Meredith laughed. "Give me the coin," she said, "and come on downstairs. It's time for that program about deep-sea divers looking for the wrecks of old treasure ships."

9

Meredith woke up early on Saturday. She was out of bed and dressed before her mother came to call her. When she came downstairs Christopher was already eating breakfast.

"One of the kids at school told me he found a cave in the park," Christopher said.

Meredith looked out of the window at the blue sky. "I wonder if there are any baby ducks on the lake." She sat down at the kitchen table and filled a bowl with shredded wheat.

Mrs. Dalby poured milk into the bowl. "Why don't you two go to the park today? The magnolias must be in bloom."

After breakfast Meredith ran up to her room. She tucked the silver coin into the pocket of her jeans. It might come in handy in the park, she thought. She put on a light jacket and went to find Christopher.

He was in his room, going through the drawers of his desk. "Here it is!" He held up a little fishing drop-line. "Dad says he read in the paper that the lake has been freshly stocked with fish."

"Get your jacket on," Meredith said, "and let's go."

Christopher's jacket was hanging on the back of a chair. He picked it up and put it on as he ran downstairs.

Prospect Park was five blocks away. Meredith and Christopher walked down Ocean Parkway and went into the park by the corner gate.

There were big sticky buds on the horse chestnut trees and little green spikes poking out of the ground. The children crossed the road that wound through the park. No cars were allowed there on weekends. The road was full of people riding bicycles, pushing baby carriages, roller-skating, and jogging.

Four teenagers on horseback were coming down the bridle path. Meredith and Christopher waited until they had galloped past. Then they walked across to the grassy slope above the lake.

Meredith ran down to the stone wall that bordered the water. She saw two brown ducks and one with a beautiful green head swimming on the lake. But there weren't any ducklings.

Meredith started walking along the wall. Christopher followed her. They passed a man who was fishing. Only children were allowed to fish in the park, but older people often did.

Around a bend of the lake they came to a place where there was a tangle of water lily plants in the water. There were no flowers there yet, but Christopher remembered that he had once seen a fish swimming among the floating stems. He put his hand into his pocket to take out the drop-line.

"Hey, kid, let's see what you've got in your pocket." Two big boys stepped out of the woods near the lake. One of them yanked at Christopher's hand.

Christopher pulled out the drop-line.

The boy looked at it. "I don't need that piece of junk. What else have you got in your pockets, kid?"

Christopher felt in his pockets. He took out a battered piece of red crayon and a green plastic pencil sharpener.

The other boy looked at Meredith. "Maybe the girl has something."

Meredith could have run away, but she didn't want to leave Christopher. She put her hand in her pocket. There was just one thing in there—the magic coin. She held it out.

The boy grabbed it. "What do you know? Here's a quarter!"

The first boy came over to take a look. "Stupid! That's no quarter." He snatched the coin and dropped it into the murky water of the lake.

The two big boys ran back into the woods.

10

As soon as the two big boys had gone, Meredith kneeled down on the stone wall at the edge of the lake. She looked into the water. Something round and shiny caught her eye.

Meredith slipped out of her jacket and laid it on the wall. She took off her shoes and socks and rolled up her jeans. Then she stepped into the lake. The water was much deeper than she had thought it was. It came almost up to her waist. "Ouch!"

"What's the matter?" Christopher asked.

"There's all sorts of stuff on the bottom of the lake," Meredith told him. "I stubbed my toe."

"You should have kept your shoes on," Christopher said.

Meredith leaned over and felt around in the slime near her feet. She fished up a little metal circle. "What's this?"

Christopher looked at it. "That's the pop-top from a beer can."

Meredith was soaking wet. The

water was much colder than the air. "The coin must be right here. I saw just where that nasty kid dropped it."

Her teeth were chattering, but Meredith went on looking for the silver coin. She started pulling things out of the lake. She found three more pop-tops, a plastic bag with half a rotten orange in it, a green woolen mitten, and a Coca Cola bottle. Her feet were getting colder and colder.

Meredith was about to give up looking when she felt something hard under her left foot. She reached down and dug it out of the mud. "Look!"

"It's Juan Pablo! Now you'd better get out of that water." Christopher held out his hand. Meredith grabbed hold of it.

Christopher pulled as hard as he could. The wall was slippery. His feet skidded out from under him.

Splash! Christopher fell into the lake beside Meredith.

They tried to climb onto the stone wall. It was covered with soft green scum, and they couldn't get a grip on it.

Meredith held onto the silver coin. "My feet are freezing."

"It feels like winter." Christopher looked across the lake. "But I know it's spring. Those people over there are rowing a boat. And the park doesn't rent boats in the winter."

"I wish we were in a boat," Meredith said. "Then maybe my feet wouldn't be so cold."

She felt the coin move in her hand. "Chris," Meredith whispered, "Juan Pablo's up to his tricks again!"

Christopher blinked. He saw that Meredith was still holding onto the edge of what must be the coin. But it had spread itself down and under and around them.

Meredith and Christopher were in a little silver rowboat.

They sat down on the seat. Christopher pointed to the floor. "That Juan Pablo thinks of everything!"

Meredith saw two silver oars lying side by side in the bottom of the boat.

11

The silver boat was close to the stone wall at the edge of the lake. Meredith took her jacket and shoes and socks off the wall. She put them on. "Now I feel better."

"But I don't," Christopher said. "My shoes and jacket are just as wet as everything else I'm wearing."

"In the television program we saw last night the divers looking for treasure were wet all over," Meredith said.

"They didn't seem to mind."

"Don't be funny, Meredith. You know that was a warm sea," Christopher said. "I wish we were back in the days of treasure ships."

The boat began to swing around. Meredith picked up an oar and tried to steer it. But the little silver boat acted as if it were caught in a whirlpool. Meredith was afraid the oar would be yanked out of her hands. Christopher grabbed hold of it and helped her pull it back into the boat.

Now the boat started spinning like a top. It went so fast that the trees on the lake shore blended with the sky into a greeny-blue blur.

Meredith and Christopher got down in the bottom of the boat. They held onto each other to keep from being pitched out into the water. The boat turned faster and faster.

Meredith felt dizzy. She closed her eyes. The boat went on turning, but after a while it began to go slower. The air was getting warmer.

Meredith opened her eyes. The silver boat had stopped spinning. It rocked gently on a blue sea. Across the water Meredith could see tall cliffs rising.

"We're not in the park." Christopher climbed back onto the seat of the boat. "I wonder where we are."

Meredith slipped out of her jacket and sat down beside him. "It's so hot our clothes ought to dry in no time."

Christopher took off his jacket too. "Let's row over to the shore."

Meredith helped him fit an oar into the oarlock. Then he gave her a hand with the other oar. They began to row toward the cliffs.

Meredith leaned over the side of the boat and looked down into the clear water. "It's not very deep. I can see the bottom."

Christopher stopped rowing and stared into the water. "That looks like a zebra fish. I saw one like it in the Coney Island aquarium."

"Those rocks look mighty sharp. Maybe they're made of coral. Columbus wrecked one of his ships on a coral reef. We don't want to put a hole in our boat." Meredith steered carefully between the rocks.

The cliffs were farther away than they seemed. Christopher and Meredith rowed for more than an hour before they came close to them. They went along the shore looking for a place to land.

On the other side of a pile of rocks Meredith steered the silver boat into a little inlet. They rowed between vine-covered banks until the inlet widened into a lagoon. A white beach shaded by palm trees curved along one side of it.

"This is a great place to go swimming. Help me get the boat onto the beach, Chris." Meredith pulled off her shoes and socks and stepped out of the boat.

Christopher took off everything but his undershorts and jumped into the warm water. He dog-paddled around the boat. Then he helped Meredith drag it up onto the sand.

Christopher ran over to one of the palm trees. "Guess what I found!"

Meredith was still holding onto the boat. Now she let go of it. At once it started to shrink. A moment later Meredith couldn't see the boat anymore.

12

Christopher came running over with a big coconut. "What are you doing?"

Meredith was on her hands and knees in front of a pile of clothes and shoes.

"Where's the boat?" Christopher looked around for it.

Meredith picked up a shoe and shook it. She put it down on the sand apart from the other clothes. Then she felt in the pockets of Christopher's shirt. She laid it on top of the shoe when she had finished. Meredith looked through each piece of clothing and then moved it from one pile to the next. At last there was only one blue sock left in the first pile. "Cross your fingers, Chris."

Christopher crossed his fingers and

held his breath. He watched Meredith squeeze the sock. There was nothing in it. Meredith laid the sock on top of the rest of the clothes.

"Look!" Christopher pointed to something shiny that was almost buried in the sand.

Meredith reached for it. "Juan Pablo!" She held the magic coin against her cheek. "I was afraid it was just another pop-top," she told Christopher.

"He must have gotten tired of being a boat," Christopher said. "I'm glad he's still with us."

Meredith put the coin deep in the pocket of her jeans. "Where'd you find the coconut, Chris?"

"There are a lot on the ground under those trees. I wonder how we can get it open," Christopher said.

"Give it to me." Meredith put the coconut on a flat rock. She started to pick up a large stone. It was too heavy for her to lift.

Christopher grabbed one end of the stone. Together they held it over the rock. "One, two, three, wham!" Christopher said.

Crack! The coconut split in two. A sticky juice splashed across the rock and spurted onto the two children. They set the stone on the ground.

Meredith dipped her fingers in the juice inside one of the pieces of coconut. She sucked them. "Not bad."

Christopher started to drink the juice out of the other piece of coconut.

It was a different sort of picnic and rather messy. Their faces were sticky from dipping them into the coconut shells. When they'd eaten all they wanted, Meredith said, "Let's go swimming. It's an easy way to get our faces washed."

She took off her shirt and her jeans and put them in the pile of clothes on the beach. She checked to make sure the silver coin was safe in her pocket. Then, wearing her undershirt and pants, she waded into the blue water of the bay.

Christopher splashed in after her.

The water was so clear that they could see their feet on the white sand. A school of bright-colored little fish swam around Meredith's ankles. She waded until the water was above her knees. Then she started to swim.

Swimming always seemed like flying to Meredith. She rolled over and drifted along on her back.

Christopher was swimming underwater. He came up for air. "I'll race you to that big rock in the water."

Meredith turned back onto her stomach and swam toward the rock. Christopher got to it first. He climbed up and sat next to the bush. Meredith pulled herself out of the water and lay down in the sun.

The rock was smooth and warm. Meredith closed her eyes. Christopher stretched out next to her. Both of them fell fast asleep.

13

When Meredith opened her eyes it was very dark. For a moment she didn't remember where she was. She looked up at a sky that seemed to have more stars than she had ever seen in her life. And she could hear the waves slapping against the rock.

Christopher was curled up beside her on the rock. Meredith reached over and touched his shoulder. "Chris, wake up!"

Christopher sat up and stretched. "It's late! We'd better go home."

"Mother must be worried." Meredith stood up. Her eyes were getting used to the darkness. She could see the white beach gleaming in the starlight.

"What did you do with Juan Pablo?" Christopher asked.

"He's in the pocket of my jeans. We have to get our clothes." Meredith slipped off the rock into the water. She swam toward the beach. Christopher came after her.

The beach seemed much bigger now that they had to find their clothes in the dark. "I wish I could remember just where we left them," Meredith said.

They started crisscrossing the beach, walking away from each other. Meredith bent down and felt the sand whenever she came to a shadow. She was afraid she'd pass right by the pile of clothes.

It was Christopher who found them. He let out a whoop of joy. "Get dressed, Meredith, and ask Juan Pablo to take us home."

Meredith ran over and picked up her jeans. She felt in her pocket for the silver coin. It was right where she had left it.

All the clothes were dry now. Christopher and Meredith put them on over their wet underwear. They pulled on their socks and shoes and tied their jackets around their waists.

Meredith took out the magic coin and held it up in the starlight. "Please, Juan Pablo," she said, "take us home."

Nothing happened.

It was too dark to see the little bearded face on the coin. Meredith wondered if Juan Pablo was angry.

But she had no way of knowing.

"Juan Pablo," Christopher said, "can't you turn yourself back into a boat and sail us home again?"

Still nothing happened.

"I guess he's mad at us. Let's see if we can find another coconut. I'm hungry." Christopher walked toward the palm trees.

Meredith didn't want to lose Christopher in the dark. She ran after him. She was hungry too, and there was a faint smell drifting by on the breeze that made her even hungrier. She caught up to her brother and grabbed his arm. "Chris, somebody's cooking something."

Christopher sniffed the air. "Let's follow our noses and see what we can find."

They went slowly, trying to follow the scent. Meredith pretended she was a bloodhound. The smell reminded her of roast beef. Her mouth started to water.

"It's coming from the woods," Christopher said.

Meredith didn't like being in the woods after dark even when they went to the country in the summertime. And these woods were almost like a jungle. But she was so hungry now that her stomach hurt. "I wish we had a flashlight."

She felt the coin in her hand move. It was getting bigger and changing shape. Meredith ran her fingers over it. Click! A little beam of light lit the darkness.

Christopher turned around. "Juan Pablo's turned himself into a flashlight." He grinned. "I guess he isn't mad anymore."

14

Meredith shined the flashlight at the tangled woods. "Look, Chris. There's a path!"

A narrow track had been made through the vines and bushes on the ground. It looked new. The twigs and branches on each side of it were broken but still green and leafy.

They walked single file. Meredith was in front with the flashlight. The light attracted a big moth. Suddenly, out of the darkness, something came flapping down. It brushed against Meredith's arm and then crashed back into the woods.

Meredith jumped back. "What kind of bird do you think that was?"

"It went so fast I couldn't get a good look at it," Christopher told her. "Maybe it was a bat."

A bat seemed much spookier than a bird. The woods were full of scary shadows and even scarier noises.

They heard a harsh sort of chirp. Then a gray lizard darted across the path in front of them.

Meredith kept walking. She was beginning to be frightened, but she didn't want Christopher to know it.

The cooking smell was stronger now. Smoke drifted between the trees. Meredith wondered if the woods were on fire. Maybe they should run back to the beach before they were trapped.

"Listen!" Christopher said. "Somebody's singing!"

Meredith heard a man's voice and the plinking of a guitar. She started walking faster. The path was going uphill now. The singing sounded closer, and the smoke was thicker. It curled down the path like a fog and made Meredith's eyes sting.

At the top of the hill they looked down into a clearing in the woods. There was a row of smoky fires with wooden racks stretched over them. The racks must be covered with cooking meat, Meredith thought. The smell was so strong now that she could hardly stand it.

The fires gave enough light for Meredith and Christopher to see two men sitting cross-legged on the ground. The row of fires was in front of the men, and the wind blew from behind them. The smoke was blowing away from them and toward the children.

There were hardly any trees on this side of the hill, but there were a lot of short stumps. "I guess the trees were cut for firewood," Christopher said.

An orange moon began to rise above the trees. It gave a murky glow to the smoke and gleamed on the bare, stony hillside.

Meredith turned off the flashlight. She felt it shrink in her hand. In the moonlight she could see that she was once more holding the silver coin. She put it back into the pocket of her jeans.

They started down the steep hillside. Their feet sent the stones underfoot rolling down. Meredith and Christopher grabbed onto the stumps to keep from sliding.

The man had stopped singing. When the children reached the bottom of the hill they stepped over to the fires and looked through the smoke at the two men.

One man was very tall. He had a red beard and wore a blue scarf tied around his head. The other was shorter. His hair and beard were gray, and he had a gold earring in one ear. Both men were wearing baggy pants and short floppy boots. They were standing up now. The tall man had a curved sword in his hand, and the other one held a big pistol.

Christopher moved closer to Meredith. "They're pirates!" he whispered.

15

The two men stared at Meredith and Christopher.

"Who else is with you?" the man with the red beard asked.

"Nobody," Meredith told him. "We're all alone."

"Come here, lass," the other man said.

Meredith started to walk slowly between two of the smoky fires toward the men.

The gray-haired man looked at Christopher. "You too, lad."

Christopher rushed after Meredith and grabbed hold of her hand. She took a deep breath and marched over to the fierce-looking men.

The men were still holding the gun and the sword. They kept looking up the hill as if they expected somebody to come out of the woods on the top.

At last the older man put the big pistol in his belt. "You really do seem to be alone. How did you come here?"

"In a boat," Christopher said. "We rowed into the bay."

"You mean the lagoon I suppose." The tall man with the red beard laid his sword down. "They must have been in a ship's dinghy," he said to his friend. He turned to Meredith. "There are vipers in the woods, lass. You might have been bitten in the dark.

Why did you come here to our camp?"

Meredith decided not to tell him about the flashlight. "We haven't had anything but a coconut to eat since breakfast," she said. "We smelled your meat cooking. It smelled better when we weren't so close to it."

"The smell does get powerful," the tall man agreed. "We've gotten used to it."

"How will you ever eat all this meat?" Christopher asked.

The gray-haired man laughed. "We're not cooking the meat to eat it, lad. We're smoking it so it will keep for months on a sea voyage." He smiled at Christopher. His face didn't look fierce now. "What's your name?"

"Christopher. This is my sister, Meredith."

"You can call me Jonathan," the gray-haired man said. "My friend here is Matt."

"We've plenty of stew left from supper, Meredith," Matt said. "You and your brother are welcome to it."

"Thank you." Meredith followed Matt to a big iron pot that was hanging over the glowing embers of a small fire. Christopher came over to join her.

Matt filled two reddish-brown pottery bowls with warm stew. He gave one to each of the children.

They sat side by side on a log and ate with their fingers. The stew tasted different from what their mother made, but it was good. They licked their fingers clean.

"The water barrel is over by our cottage." Matt pointed to a hut made of palm branches.

Christopher and Meredith walked over to the barrel. There was no cup. They drank out of a long-handled dipper.

Christopher wiped his mouth with the back of his hand. "Let's go see what Jonathan is doing."

Jonathan was walking from one big fire to the next. He poked at the firewood with a pointed stick. "If I don't give the fires air, they'll die out."

Meredith looked at the wood. "It's still green," she said. "I thought firewood had to be dry."

"That's why the fire smokes," Jonathan said. "It's a trick we learned from the Indians around here. They dry the meat in the sun and then smoke it. That way it keeps without salt."

"Indians?" Christopher said. "Around here?" He turned to look at the shadows beyond the fires.

"There are still some left, but not nearly as many as there were a few years ago," Jonathan told him. "Let's talk about you now. Where are your parents?"

16

"Mom and Dad are home in Brooklyn," Christopher said.

Jonathan rubbed his gray beard. "Do you mean the little town by the New York harbor? I once sailed on a ship that docked there. You're a long way from home."

"And we don't know how to get back," Meredith said.

"How did you get here?" Jonathan wanted to know.

"Juan Pablo brought us," Christopher told him. "But he won't take us home again."

"You can't trust some of these sea captains," Jonathan said. "But don't worry, young ones. We will get you home. There's bound to be a ship going to New York to get a cargo of wheat flour. That's something they pay well for in these parts." Jonathan gave another poke to the smoky fire. "I'm tired. These fires will last till morning. Come along. We'll rig up a roost for you."

Jonathan picked up a burning stick and walked toward the little hut. Meredith and Christopher started after him.

They passed the water barrel. Matt was leaning against it, smoking a pipe. Jonathan was at the low doorway of the hut. He ducked his head to go through it. Meredith and Christopher came in after him.

Matt knocked the ashes out of his pipe. He took hold of the water barrel and backed into the little house, leaving the barrel to block the doorway.

Jonathan lit a thick candle from the

burning stick. He put the stick on the dirt floor and stamped out the fire with his boots. Then he stuck the candle in a bottle and set it on the ground. He walked over to what looked like a pile of fishing nets. He tied one end of a net to a pole in a corner of the hut and the other end to a pole in the middle of the floor.

"It's a hammock!" Christopher said.

Meredith looked around the little room. There was hardly space for four hammocks. "Why don't we sleep outside?"

"Herds of wild animals are roaming around in the hills," Matt told her. "The fire will most likely keep them away from the camp, but it's better not to take chances."

Christopher thought for a minute. "Wild animals in herds, are they deer or buffalo?"

Matt laughed. "These are herds of cattle, goats, and pigs."

"Those aren't wild animals," Christopher said.

"The grandparents of these animals lived on farms," Matt told him. "But when the Spaniards left this place, the animals they left behind ran wild."

Jonathan strung up four hammocks. Each went from a corner pole to one in the center of the hut. "Time for bed."

The two men took off their leather boots and belts. The gun and the sword went into the hammocks with them when they lay down.

Meredith and Christopher decided to sleep in their clothes too. They even left their shoes on.

When they were all snug in their hammocks, Jonathan leaned over the edge of his and blew out the candle.

Meredith lay in the dark and wondered if her mother were calling the hospitals to find out if she and Christopher had been in an accident. Meredith wasn't as tired as she would have been if she hadn't taken the long nap on the rock. Long before she fell asleep she heard Matt and Jonathan begin to snore.

"Meredith," Christopher whispered, "isn't it lucky we did all our homework last night? Now we don't have anything to worry about."

17

Meredith was worried about a lot of things. After Christopher was asleep she tossed and turned in her hammock. She was used to seeing people in strange clothes. In Brooklyn sometimes they even shaved their heads and wore long robes. But Matt and Jonathan looked like something out of a movie. And their speech sounded different from anything Meredith had ever heard. It was just as if they belonged to a long ago time.

What had Christopher said to make the silver boat start to spin? The spinning had made Meredith so dizzy that she couldn't remember.

When at last she fell asleep Meredith slept till morning. She woke to the sound of someone shouting.

"Ahoy! Anybody here?" a deep voice bellowed.

Jonathan rolled out of his hammock and reached over to shake Matt. He pulled on his boots and buckled his belt. Then he picked up the big pistol. He crouched low and moved over to the doorway of the hut. He rested the pistol on the water barrel that blocked the bottom of the doorway and peered over it.

Matt was up and ready in an instant. He grabbed the curved sword and stood on one side of the doorway.

"Ahoy!" The voice yelled even

louder. "You're getting to be a lazy landlubber. The sun's been up for hours."

"That sounds like Talbot," Matt whispered.

"Best to be sure," Jonathan whispered back. He kept his gun ready and shouted out the top of the doorway. "Who's there?"

"Is that you, Jonathan?" the voice asked. "Jeremy Talbot here."

"What's at the bottom of the apple barrel?" Matt called out.

"Peanuts," the voice answered.

At this Jonathan stuck the pistol in his belt. Matt put down the curved sword. Together they pushed the heavy water barrel out of the doorway. Then the two men ran out of the hut.

Both Meredith and Christopher were wide awake now. They climbed out of their hammocks and went to see what was going on.

They found Jonathan and Matt taking turns hugging a short, stocky man.

Jonathan caught sight of the children. "Come over here, young ones. I want you to meet an old friend of mine."

Meredith and Christopher walked over to the three men.

"Jem," Jonathan said, "this is Meredith and her brother, Christopher. They hail from Brooklyn town. They came to these parts with a sea captain who left them high and dry. I'd like to get them on a ship for home."

Meredith held out her hand. "How do you do."

Jem shook her hand and then Christopher's. Like Jonathan and Matt he was wearing boots. He had on a blue shirt that was open at the neck, a red sash around his waist, and baggy blue pants with red stripes on them. His dark hair was cut short and was turning gray. He had lumpy ears, a crooked nose, and teeth that were stained and broken. But there was a twinkle in his green eyes and something nice about his smile. Both of the children liked him at once.

"I was hoping you'd still be here," he said to Matt and Jonathan. "Have you given up the sea for good?"

"We've got a good trade," Matt said. "The Spaniards left their livestock roaming around, so there's plenty of meat. And the ships around here will buy as much as we can dry. We could use help. Why don't you join us? It's safer than seafaring."

"Thanks for your offer," Jem said. "I'd like to work with you, but I signed on as a mate with a privateer. He's agreed to give me a share of the profits when the ship reaches port. If I got some money together I'd start a sugar plantation on this island. Then I could bring my family over from England."

"If anything goes wrong," Matt told him, "you're welcome here. And you can make a living for your family smoking meat."

Jem smiled. "I'll remember that," he said.

18

"Captain Bardfield is loading *The Red Goose* for a voyage," Jem said. "I'm sure he'll buy your dried meat. Can you get some ready?"

"Where's the ship?" Jonathan asked.

"She's anchored out beyond the reefs. I came ashore on the longboat. The men are waiting on the beach for me." Jem turned to Meredith and Christopher. "I'll ask the captain to let you sail with us. If we don't head for your port, we'll put you on a ship that's going that way."

Christopher was excited. "What kind of ship is *The Red Goose?*"

Jem smiled. "She's at least a hundred and fifty tons. And she carries ten guns and a crew of twenty."

"That's a good-sized ship," Matt said.

Jem was looking at Meredith. "I don't mean to be rude," he said, "but aren't you wearing boys' clothes?"

"Of course she is," Jonathan said. "You don't think little girls in Brooklyn go around dressed like that. The lass has been at sea for a long time." He looked hard at the blue jeans Christopher and Meredith were wearing. "But you can see they've got a different style of clothing in that part of the world."

Matt walked over to where the iron pot was hanging. He started to poke the dead embers with a stick.

Meredith grabbed Christopher by the hand. "We're going to help Matt," she told Jonathan. She pulled her brother away from the two men. "I have to talk to you when we're alone," she whispered.

Matt sent Christopher to gather firewood and gave Meredith a jug to fill from the water barrel. When he got a jug of water boiling, he poured oats from a big cloth bag into it.

"Did you ever milk a goat?" Matt asked Meredith.

She shook her head.

"Come along. I'll teach you how." Matt picked up a wooden pail and walked across to the woods at the edge of the clearing.

Meredith followed him. When they came to the trees she saw two donkeys roped to one of them. A goat and a young kid, a baby goat, were tied to another.

"This is Eleanor and her son Fred,"

Matt told her. He squatted down on his heels beside the goat and put the pail under her. "Good morning, Eleanor." He patted the goat. "How about giving us a little milk for breakfast."

When Matt had finished milking the goat he took a sweet potato out of the front of his shirt and gave it to her.

Meredith reached out to pet the kid. Matt grabbed her hand to stop her.

"Better not. Eleanor might take a bite out of you." He picked up the pail of foaming milk. "Let's go see if the porridge is ready."

After breakfast all three men began to tie slabs of smoked meat together and pile them into baskets that hung on both sides of the donkeys. The meat was stiff and dry and looked as hard as wood.

When the donkeys were loaded with as much as they could carry, Matt handed Christopher a bundle of meat. "Is this too heavy for you?"

"I'll manage," Christopher said.

Matt gave a bundle to Meredith. "Try carrying it on your head. That's what the people around here do."

Meredith lifted the bundle onto her head. It was easier to carry that way. Christopher decided to do the same thing. Then each of the three men picked up a large bundle of dried meat and balanced it on top of his head. Jonathan and Matt had ropes to the donkeys tied around their waists.

Jem went first up the stump-covered hill. Matt and Jonathan followed with the donkeys. Meredith and Christopher came after them, holding the heavy bundles on their heads with both hands.

19

Meredith wanted to talk to Christopher, but they had to walk so fast to keep up with the men and the donkeys that there wasn't time.

The woods looked different in the daytime. Green parrots flew from one tree to the next. And vines covered with bright red flowers hung from the branches.

The piles of dried meat seemed to get heavier and heavier as they marched along the narrow path through the forest. Just as Meredith was sure she'd have to stop and rest, they came to a grove of tall palm trees.

The next minute Meredith stepped out into the sunlight on the sandy beach.

A long wooden boat was pulled up out of the water. There were groups of men sitting wherever there was a patch of shade. They were smoking pipes and playing cards.

One man stood up and walked toward them. He had on a ruffled shirt, and his hair was almost as long as Meredith's. It curled over a lace collar. Meredith saw jewels in the hilt of his sword. "I'm glad to see you, Talbot," he said to Jem. "You were gone so long I was afraid something had happened to you."

Jem took the bundle off his head. "Captain," he said, "my friends here have been drying meat in the Indian manner. I told them you'd buy a load for the ship."

"Good day, gentlemen," the captain

said. "Let's see what you have here." He took a good look at the meat Jem was carrying. "Excellent. Do you want to be paid in coin or in goods? I can give you cloth and tea and good Dutch cheese. And of course we're well stocked with molasses, sugar, and rum."

"We can use supplies, sir," Jonathan said, "but for the most part we'd like to be paid in gold."

"Very well." The captain talked about the price with Jonathan and Matt. Then he took a leather purse from inside his shirt and gave an equal number of gold coins to each of them.

Jonathan put his gold in a little bag that hung around his neck. Matt rolled his in a red handkerchief and tied it to his belt.

"Ahoy, coxswain," the captain called.

One of the men playing cards stood up.

"Row these men out to the ship with this meat. See that they get the supplies they need."

Jonathan and Matt helped the coxswain push the longboat into the water. Three sailors unloaded the donkeys. Meredith and Christopher went to put their bundles in the boat.

"Come over here, children," Jem called.

They ran back to where he was standing beside the captain.

"These are the young people I was telling you about," he said. "Meredith and Christopher, I want you to meet Captain Bardfield."

Meredith held out her hand. "How do you do."

The captain bowed. He shook first her hand and then Christopher's. "I understand you hail from Brooklyn town. I've a cargo of rum that should sell for a good price there. You can sail along with me, and you can earn your way by working in the ship's galley."

"Thank you, Captain Bardfield," Meredith said.

20

Meredith and Christopher watched as the coxswain and three other men rowed Jonathan and Matt across the lagoon. The longboat went into the little inlet and disappeared from sight.

"There are a lot of things here I don't understand," Christopher said.

"Neither did I at first," Meredith told him.

"I thought Jonathan and Matt were pirates," Christopher said, "but they turned out to be really nice guys. All these other people look like pirates too. They just don't act like them. Captain Bardfield could get a job acting in *Peter Pan* if he had a hook instead of a hand."

"Chris," Meredith said, "don't you

know there aren't any pirates nowadays? And if there were they wouldn't dress like this and carry swords."

Christopher didn't say anything for a minute. When he spoke it was in a scared whisper. "Meredith, what does it all mean?"

Meredith sat down on the sand and started to build a castle. "I'm still not sure, Chris, and I don't want to worry you until I am. Help me dig this moat."

Christopher dug down so far that the moat filled with sea water. The children used the water to pack the sand into a big tower. They built a wall with a turret on each corner and put sea shells on all the pointed roofs.

"That's a beautiful castle." They looked up into Jem's twinkly green eyes. "Too bad we can't stay here and live in it," he said, "but the longboat's coming back across the lagoon. It's time to head for the open sea."

Meredith and Christopher stood up. They followed Jem to where the long-boat was being pulled up onto the beach.

Matt and Jonathan got out of the boat. They carried barrels and bags over to the donkeys who were tied up in the shade of a palm tree. Then the two men ran back to the boat. Christopher and Meredith were sitting in it next to Jem.

Jonathan put his arms around the children and hugged them. "If you run into trouble, you can always come back to us."

"Eleanor will let you stroke Fred when she gets to know you," Matt told Meredith. "Take care of the young ones," he said to Jem, "and remember what I told you."

The sailors started to shove the boat into the water.

"All ashore that's going ashore," the coxswain bellowed.

Matt and Jonathan jumped out of the boat. They waded up onto the beach and stood there watching as it was rowed across the lagoon. Meredith and Christopher waved to them until the boat went into the inlet.

There were ten men rowing the boat. They pulled it through the water with long sure strokes. It went past the vine-covered banks and came to the sea. Then the boat started to glide between the sharp rocks of the coral reef.

Meredith looked across the open water. She saw a tall sailing ship moored out beyond the reef. It had three masts and a high stern. And it looked something like pictures she had seen of the ship the Pilgrim Fathers sailed in.

"Chris," she whispered. "Look! Now do you understand?"

Christopher stared. "We're back in the days of the treasure ships. Isn't that great?"

"Not really," Meredith said.

"What do you mean?" Christopher asked.

"When we get to Brooklyn we still won't be home," Meredith told him. "Mother and Daddy won't even be born for hundreds of years."

21

After the longboat had safely crossed the reef it was rowed over to the sailing ship.

"Ahoy!" the coxswain yelled.

Someone high above on the deck of the ship tossed a rope ladder over the side. Captain Bardfield was the first to climb it.

"You go next, Meredith." Jem helped her onto the bottom rung.

Meredith held tight to the ropes on each side of the wooden rungs. It took her a moment or two to get used to the swaying ladder. Then she started up. When she got to the top, a sailor pulled her over the side of the ship onto the deck.

Christopher followed Meredith up the ladder. Jem climbed up after him.

"Come with me." Jem took the children down a narrow stairway and along a hall to the ship's kitchen.

A tubby little man with white hair and pink cheeks was peeling onions. He looked up. "Hello, Jem."

"These are your new helpers, Meredith and Christopher. They haven't had lunch, and neither have I." Jem turned to the children. "This is Barnaby, the ship's cook. He'll tell you what to do."

Barnaby put a round orange cheese on the table beside a crusty loaf of bread. He handed Jem a knife. "Help yourselves. There are apples in the barrel over there."

When they had finished eating, Jem went back down the hall. Barnaby set Meredith to work peeling the onions, but they made her eyes water. He gave her the job of scouring a copper saucepan with white beach sand. Christopher peeled the onions. They didn't make him cry.

The saucepan was shining like a new penny when Meredith heard a loud grating sound. The ship gave a sudden lurch.

Meredith put down the pan. "What happened? Is the ship sinking?"

Barnaby laughed. "They're hoisting the anchor. You two have done enough work for now. Why don't you go up on deck and watch? I'll send for you if I've got anything for you to do."

Christopher and Meredith raced down the hall and up the stairs. Six strong-looking sailors were singing and turning a big wheel that was mounted flat on the deck. As the wheel turned, the heavy rope to the anchor was wound around it, and the anchor was lifted up from the ocean floor.

Sailors were climbing around in the rigging. They unfurled the sails to the wind. *The Red Goose* seemed to be spreading her wings.

Jem walked across the deck to the children. "We've caught the tide at just the right moment. Now we're on our way. I have to stand watch now. Do you want to keep me company?"

Meredith and Christopher went to the front of the ship with Jem. He brought along a brass telescope.

"Let me look through it, Jem," Christopher begged.

Jem handed him the telescope.

Christopher squinted through it and turned it slowly in all directions. "There's something shining way out there."

Jem took the telescope and looked where Christopher was pointing. He called to a sailor. "Tell the captain there's a ship off the starboard bow."

22

Captain Bardfield looked through the telescope for three full minutes. "Talbot," he said, "that's a Spanish galleon. It must be the *Cadiz*. I heard that she was in these waters, headed for Spain with a cargo of Mexican gold. We'll get as close as we can and attack first thing in the morning."

"Go below," Jem whispered to Meredith and Christopher. "Things are going to get rough."

"Jem," Meredith said, "are you a pirate?"

"I don't want to be," Jem told her in a low voice, "but the captain is in charge here. If I don't follow orders, I'll be hanged for mutiny."

"But why did you join a pirate crew?" Christopher asked.

"When there's a treasure ship in sight, any crew might turn pirate," Jem told him. He pulled the children over to the stairway that led to the lower deck. "Stay with Barnaby."

Meredith and Christopher spent the rest of the afternoon in the galley with the cook. Barnaby told them stories of his life in England.

"Why did you go to sea?" Meredith asked.

"There was no way to earn a living at home," the cook told her. "I became a soldier and fought in a war. When the war was over I had no trade to make money. I signed on a ship and sailed west."

"Were you always a cook?" Christopher wanted to know.

Barnaby puffed out his chest. "I was boatswain for twenty years," he said, "until I got rheumatism in my knees and couldn't climb the rigging to check the sails." He looked out of the small square window. "We're getting close to the Spaniard. To tell you the truth I don't like it. It would be better if the captain stuck to trading rum for flour."

Meredith saw the sky through the window. It was turning red.

The galley was getting dark, but Barnaby didn't light the lantern. "Captain's orders," he said.

At suppertime Meredith and Christopher carried pans of food to the mess hall and set them on the bare trestle tables there. The sailors ate by the dim light from the little windows.

Barnaby strung up hammocks for the children in the hall outside the galley. They went to bed before it was completely dark. Meredith was sure she'd never fall asleep, but the next thing she knew she was awakened by a loud boom.

Meredith rolled out of her hammock. "Chris, wake up! It's morning!"

Christopher blinked and sat up. "There's going to be a sea battle. I want to see it."

He ran down the hall and up the stairway to the deck. Meredith chased after him.

The Red Goose had sailed so close to the *Cadiz* that they could see the people on the Spanish ship.

The deck of the pirate ship was

crowded. Most of the sailors had swords or pistols in their hands. Some were carrying both.

Meredith ran over to Jem. "What was the bang?"

"We fired one of our cannons across the bow of the *Cadiz*," he told her. "What are you doing here, lass? I told you to stay below."

Meredith put her hands in her pockets and stood as tall as she could. "Christopher came up to see the battle. I have to stay with him." Her fingers touched the silver coin. She didn't dare take it out of her pocket here among the pirates, but she held onto it for luck.

"I never meant to mix you and your brother up in anything as nasty as this," Jem said. "I should have stayed with Matt and Jonathan."

"I wish you were with them," Meredith said.

An instant later Jem had disappeared.

"Juan Pablo," Meredith whispered, "I wish Chris and I could go back to where we belong too."

23

Meredith found herself up to her middle in icy water.

Christopher was standing beside her. He looked around. "We're back in Prospect Park. And we're still stuck in the lake. Juan Pablo is playing tricks again. I never did get to see that battle."

"I know how the coin works now, Chris." Meredith pulled the magic coin out of her pocket and held it high in the air. The silver shone in the spring sunshine.

"I *wish*," Meredith said slowly, "that Chris and I were dry and clean and standing on our own front doorstep."

She waited for something to happen.

"We're still in the lake," Christopher said. "I thought you said you knew how it works."

Meredith didn't answer him. She was thinking hard. "Maybe the magic *can't* work once you know the secret of it," she said at last.

"What do we do now then?" Christopher asked.

Meredith put the silver coin back into her pocket. She grabbed hold of the stone wall at the edge of the lake.

A young man was walking his dog by the lakeshore. "Wait a minute. Let me help you." He got down on his knees on the wall and grabbed Meredith around the waist. He lifted her out of the water. "Give me your hand," he said to Christopher and pulled him out of the lake too.

"Thank you," Meredith said.

The young man grinned. "I was always falling into the lake when I was your age. And I know how hard it is to climb out." He whistled to his dog and walked away toward the boat house.

Christopher looked across the lake. "The people in that boat over there look like the same ones I saw before. Maybe it's still Saturday!"

"Let's go home and find out." Meredith started to run. Christopher could hardly keep up with her.

They had to stop running before they got home. Both of them were out of breath.

Mrs. Dalby met them at the front door. She looked at their wet clothes and muddy shoes. "I wish there was some kind of magic that would keep you two out of trouble."

Meredith kept the silver coin safe in her pocket and went upstairs to change her clothes. She opened the bottom drawer of her desk and put the coin into it. "Thanks for everything, Juan Pablo," she said. She leaned over to take a good look at the coin.

The little bearded face was smiling.